# Usborne
# Mosaic Sticker
# Flowers

Designed and illustrated by
## Carly Davies

Written by
## Kirsteen Robson

There is a fold-out page at the back of the
book where you can try out ideas, or put your
stickers while you are not using them.

# Daisy designs

Design some daisies, then add a few fluttering butterflies.

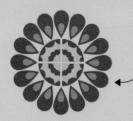

Choose stickers for the middle then stick the petals around it.

You could vary the petals or make your daisy bigger.

Side view

Here are some leaf and stem styles you could try.

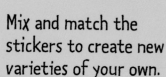

Mix and match the stickers to create new varieties of your own.

Finish your picture with tiny flowers and butterflies.

# In the meadow

Here is a grassy green meadow for you to fill with wild flowers.

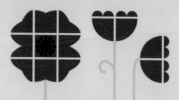 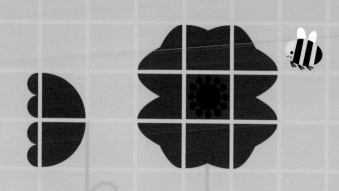

Make big or small poppies that rise above the other flowers.

You could stand your cornflowers upright or stick them on their side.

Add a few bees to the scene.

Stick leaves onto your buttercup stems.

These dandelion seeds are drifting across the meadow on a gentle breeze.

Scatter single forget-me-nots across the field, or bunch them together in groups like this.

# Cottage garden

Create a cottage garden using some of the suggestions below.

Make a sunflower that reaches the top of the page.

This flower looks like pom-poms of tiny purple petals.

Group phlox flowers and leaves like this.

Add some insects flitting from flower to flower.

Lavender bushes can grow up tall or spread sideways.

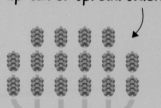

You could make some gerberas with shades of pink, or red and orange.

# Parks and gardens

Copy these ideas to show some flowers that are often planted in parks and gardens.

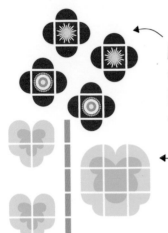

Put red, pink or white geraniums like these at the top of the page.

Add a large leaf or several small ones.

Arrange the stickers like this to make pansies.

Marigolds can be orange, red or yellow. Their sizes can vary, too.

Stick on lobelia flowers in clusters or scatter them between the other plants.

# Towering flowers

Here are some ideas for tall flowers.

Hollyhock

Add a bud or two to the top of each plant.

Stick four corners together to make round flowers.

Vary the petals on your lupin.

Add more green stickers to make taller stalks.

Bees love flowers, so add a few to your picture.

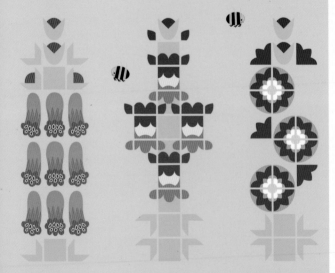

Lupin

Foxglove          Snapdragon          Delphinium

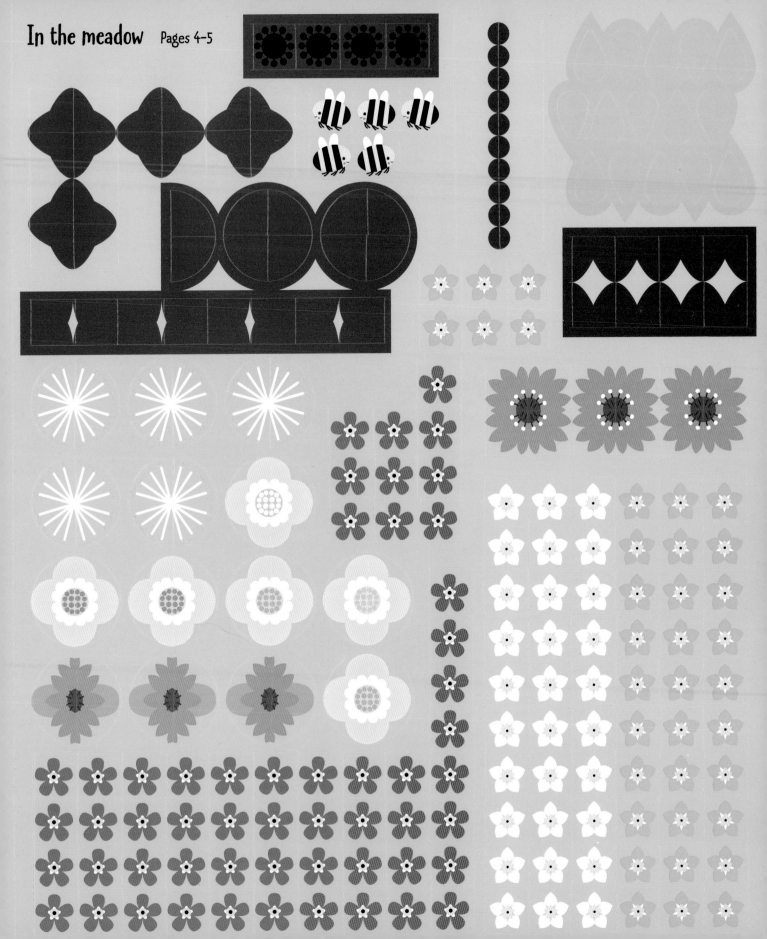

Flowers on bushes   Pages 8-9

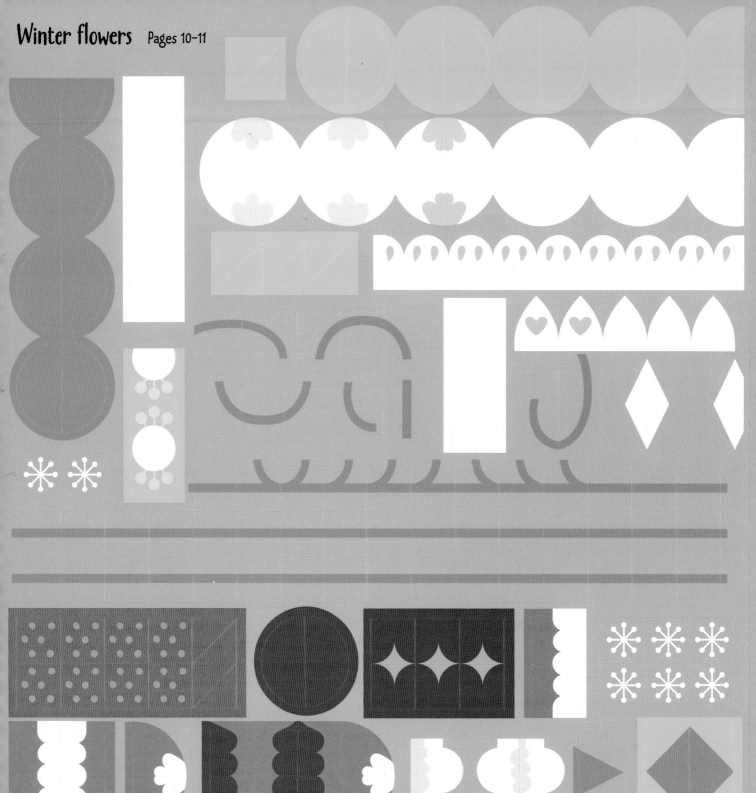

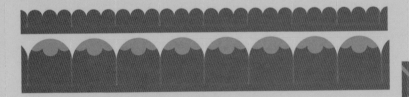

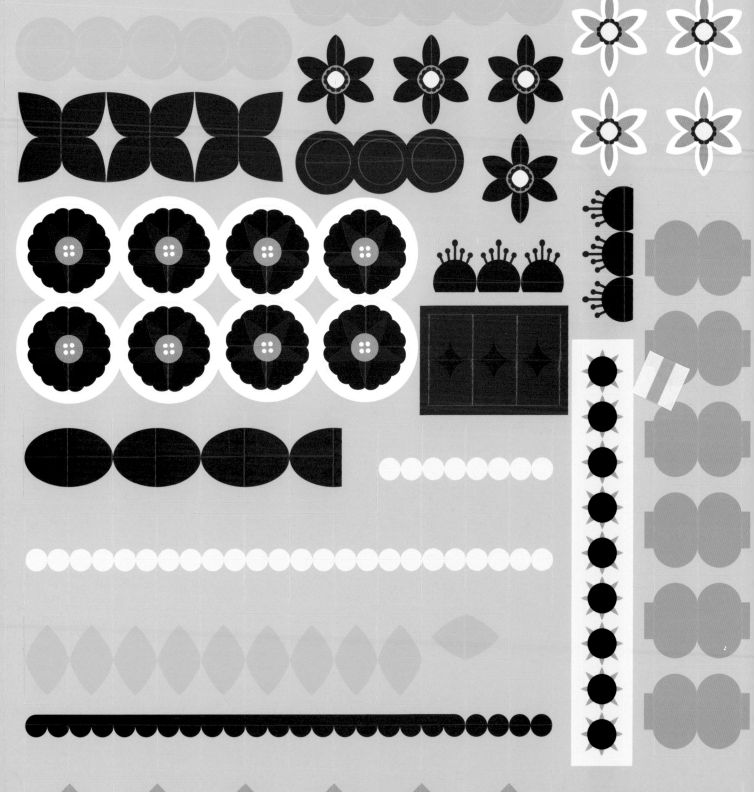

Climbers and creepers    Pages 16-17

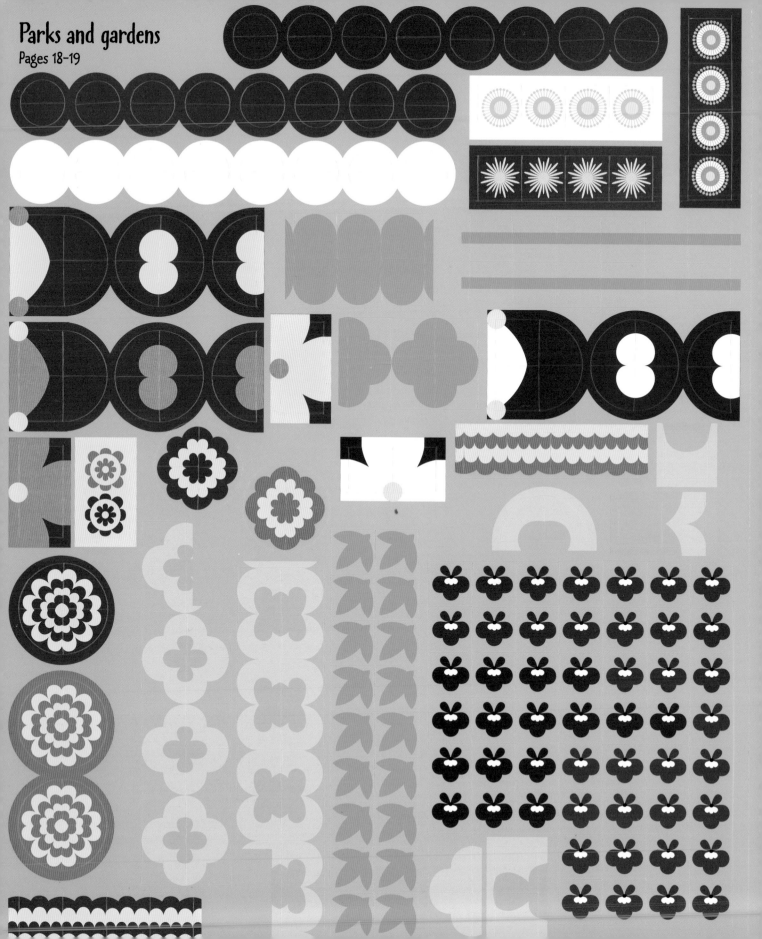

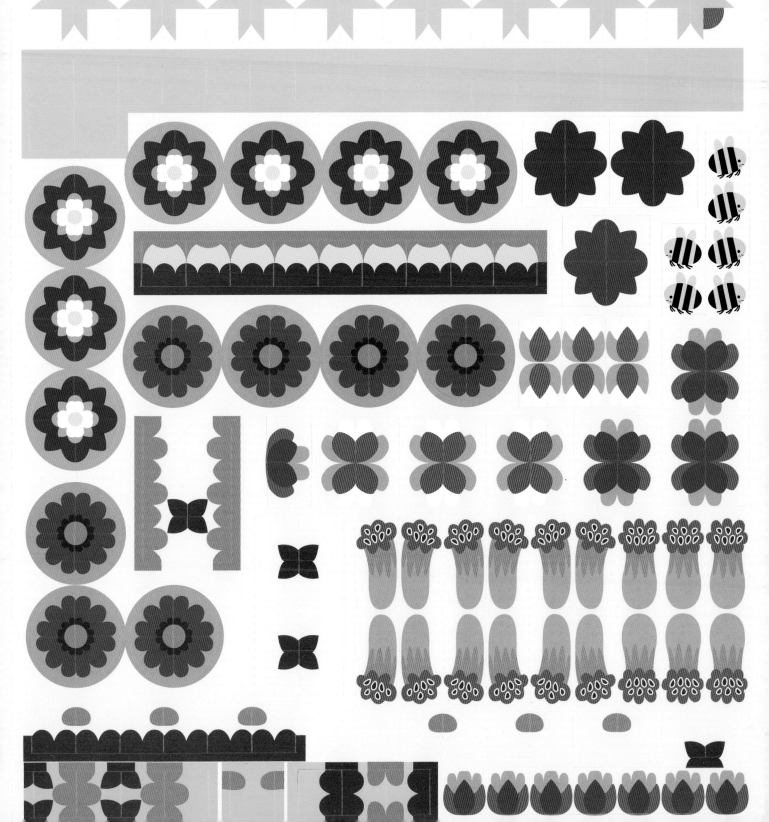